Vroom!

HOT SUVS

LINCOLN NAVIGATOR

Judy Greenspan

Rourke Educational Media

rourkeeducationalmedia.com

TABLE OF CONTENTS

LINCOLN
LINCOLN

Massive Plus Huge? That's Mahoosive!

The word "big" isn't big enough to describe the Lincoln Navigator. Try massive. Huge. Mahoosive (that means massive plus huge). Now you've got the idea.

The Lincoln **Navigator** is a mega-**luxurious** Sport Utility Vehicle, or SUV. As wide as a king-size bed and more than twice as long, this **colossal** car was created for comfortable cruising.

Stand face to **imposing** face with the Lincoln Navigator and everything screams "extra." Extra bright: double-decker jeweled headlights. Extra bold: Lincoln's signature chrome grille. Extra brash: **tinted** side windows.

When the Navigator slows down, the headlights brighten up. At night, drivers will see better on neighborhood streets.

Available in two sizes, there's extra-long too. Both Navigator models are 6.5 feet (1.9 meters) wide by 6.5 feet tall. But at a whopping 18.5 feet (5.6 meters) long, the Navigator L stretches past the standard model by more than a foot.

Big, Strong, and Fast Too

Under that extra-wide hood there's also extra strength. **Equipped** with a ferocious 450 **horsepower**, 3.5-liter engine, the Navigator has power to pull 9,000 pounds (4,082 kilograms) and can **accelerate** from 0 to 60 miles (96.5 kilometers) per hour in just 6.7 seconds.

How heavy is 9,000 pounds (4,082 kilograms)? About the same weight as nine polar bears.

How About a Hug?

Yet for all its size and strength, this burly behemoth has a light touch too. Approach the Navigator at night, key fob in hand, and suddenly your Lincoln lights up. Hello! This is the famous "Lincoln Embrace." An embrace is a hug and these welcoming lights are designed to greet you.

The "Lincoln Embrace" even turns on a lighted welcome mat. Notice the Lincoln logo too.

The front seats are modeled after seats in private airplanes.

Every living room needs comfortable chairs and the Navigator is no exception. You can adjust the front seats 30 ways. They heat up, cool down, and if you need a **massage**, they do that too.

Inside, the Navigator is roomier than most SUVs.

Inside, the "Navvie" is welcoming too. Equipped with everything from video screens, surround sound audio, and even an **optional** closet in the trunk, the Navigator has three rows of seats and plenty of room for eight people to stretch out. Some say stepping into a Lincoln Navigator is like entering "a living room on wheels."

SMART CAR

Backseat passengers have plenty of extras to keep themselves busy. Movies and TV shows are easy to watch with wireless streaming Internet and 10-inch (25.4 centimeter) screens.

Like a real navigator, the Lincoln Navigator makes getting there easy. With SYNC 3 voice-activated technology, drivers can tell the car to find a restaurant, call home, or play a favorite song. Drivers can also program the Navvie to automatically adjust the seats, steering wheel, mirrors, and even set the car's temperature.

When teens take the wheel, parents tap into technology to remind them to pay attention. Driving too fast? Radio too loud? Gas tank too low? The car chimes, beeps, and flashes safety warnings. So drive carefully, kids. The Navigator is watching.

For the best ride, drivers choose between six kinds of road conditions including "Deep" (snow, sand, mud), "Slippery" (rain, ice, dirt), and "Excite" (sport).

"L" IS FOR LINCOLN AND LUXURY

Controls for temperature and media are on the console between the seats.

A deluxe family SUV, the Lincoln Navigator comes from a long line of exceptional automobiles. For almost a century, the name "Lincoln" has meant a **lavish**, luxurious, and very expensive car.

Henry Leland started the Lincoln Motor Company in 1917. Named after President Abraham Lincoln, his company made aircraft engines during World War One. After the war, Leland began making luxury cars. Henry Ford's son, Edsel Ford, bought Lincoln Motor in 1922 and started the Ford Motor Company's luxury division. Edsel's plan? To build "the best car in the world."

Three of Lincoln's most classic models are the Zephyr, the Continental, and the Town Car. Introduced in the 1930s, the tear-shaped Zephyr had a one-piece windshield and a lightweight V-12 engine.

The name Zephyr comes from the Greek word *zephyrus*, meaning "god of the west wind."

Many famous people bought the luxurious Continental Mark II, including rock star Elvis Presley, singer Frank Sinatra, and President Dwight D. Eisenhower.

Edsel Ford
1893 – 1943

Edsel Ford treated his cars like works of art. New Lincolns were delivered to buyers in dust-free railroad cars and wrapped in large paper bags.

Called "the most beautiful car ever designed," the Lincoln Continental was custom built for Edsel in 1939. But the car was a huge hit so Edsel agreed to build 25 more in 1939 and 400 in 1940.

Introduced in 1981, the Lincoln Town Car was 18 feet (5.5 meters) long with power seats that adjusted six ways.

President Roosevelt's Sunshine Special is now on display at the Henry Ford Museum in Michigan.

Over the years, Lincoln Continentals were the cars of choice for Hollywood movie stars and many U.S. Presidents. President Franklin Delano Roosevelt's "Sunshine Special" included a siren and two-way radio. It was the first car specially built for a Commander in Chief.

E PLURIBUS UNUM

FOUR GENERATIONS

A car generation refers to changes in style and engineering.

First Generation Lincoln Navigator 1998 – 2002:

Powered by a 260-horsepower engine, the Lincoln Navigator roared onto the SUV scene in 1998. Though it had room for eight passengers, the new Navvie was shorter than the 1969-70 Lincoln Continentals.

Based on military vehicles first designed during World War II, SUVs became popular family cars in the 1990s.

Second Generation 2003 – 2006:

Known for its larger chrome grille and power running boards, the 2003 Navigator caught the eye of celebrity drivers. Hip hop mogul Sean "P. Diddy" Combs teamed up with Lincoln to design an all-black Limited Edition Sean John Navigator, with six TV screens.

In 2005, Ice Cube and the Navigator starred in the movie *Are We There Yet?*

2003 Lincoln Navigator

All third-generation models included a rear-view camera. In 2008, power-folding third-row seats were added. The standard Navigator was 17 feet (5.2 meters) long.

Third Generation 2007 – 2017:

Nearly 15 inches (38 centimeters) longer than the standard Navigator, the first Lincoln Navigator L was hard to miss.

Fourth Generation 2018 – present:

When the 2018 Navigator concept car was unveiled, car show crowds loved the enormous gull wing doors. But they didn't last past the concept.

Created for auto shows, the goal of concept cars is to test new ideas with car buyers.

What will the next Navigator look like? Kids in the back might have an intercom to call the driver up front. Or even a video-chat system. What would you dream up for the next generation?

GLOSSARY

accelerate (ak-SEL-uh-rate): to go faster and faster

colossal (kuh-LAH-suhl): extremely large

equipped (ee-KWIP-t): has the things that are needed

horsepower (HORS-pow-ur): a unit for measuring the power of an engine

imposing (im-POZE-ing): grand and impressive in appearance

lavish (LAV-ish): luxurious

luxurious (luhg-ZHOOR-ee-uhs): something expensive that's nice to have but that you don't really need

massage (muh-SAHZH): to rub someone's body to loosen their muscles, relieve pain, or help the person relax

navigator (NAV-i-gate-or): person who directs the course or route of a trip

optional (AHP-shuh-nuhl): a choice not required

tinted (TINT-ed): has a little color

INDEX

SHOW WHAT YOU KNOW

1. What is the Lincoln Embrace?
2. How long does it take for the Lincoln Navigator to go from 0 to 60 miles (96.5 kilometers) per hour?
3. What kind of vehicle did Henry Leland make during World War I?
4. What was the name of Edsel Ford's custom-designed car?
5. Which President rode in the "Sunshine Special"?

FURTHER READING

DK, *Classic Car: The Definitive Visual History, DK, 2016.*

In, Chantim, *Modern Trucks & SUVs: A Coloring Book of Trucks & Sport Utility Vehicles of Today,* CreateSpace Independent Publishing Platform, 2014.

Lacey, Saskia, and Sodomka, Martin, *How to Build a Car: A high-speed adventure of mechanics, teamwork, and friendship,* Walter Foster Jr, 2015.

ABOUT THE AUTHOR

Judy Greenspan enjoyed learning about the Lincoln Navigator and about Lincoln's elegant line of luxury automobiles. Judy lives in New York City with her family. She likes to drive but in the crowded city she always travels by train.

Meet The Author!
www.meetREMauthors.com

www.rourkeeducationalmedia.com

PHOTO CREDITS: Cover and car images pages 2 thru 19 LINCOLN MOTOR COMPANY; Header art © Petrosg; speedometer art © didis both from Shutterstock.com; Pg20-21 emperornie https://creativecommons.org/licenses/by-sa/2.0/ Thesupermat - https://creativecommons.org/licenses/by-sa/3.0/deed.en Page;22-23 Brody Levesque. - https://creativecommons.org/licenses/by-sa/4.0/deed.en Pg24 - Gen One;;Red 1998 Gen One Lincoln. Nav CR: Ford-Lincoln. Lincoln.com B/W 1971 Lincoln Cont. CR: Lincoln.com P25; Gen Two:: Black Lincoln Nav. On beach. 2003. CR: Lincoln.com PG26-27;Gen Three:: Interior 2011 Lincoln Nav. CR: Lincoln.com Rear view- Silver Lincoln Nav. -2011. CR: Lincoln.com Pg28-29; Gen Four:: Gullwing -blue Lincoln Nav-2018 Concept Car. CR: Lincoln.com Crusing Down Road - Lincoln Nav. 2018. CR: Lincoln.com

Edited by: Keli Sipperley

Cover design by: Rhea Magaro-Wallace

Library of Congress PCN Data

Lincoln Navigator / Judy Greenspan
(*VROOM!* Hot SUVs)
ISBN 978-1-64156-478-6 (hard cover)
ISBN 978-1-64156-604-9 (soft cover)
ISBN 978-1-64156-718-3 (e-Book)
Library of Congress Control Number: 2018930698

Rourke Educational Media
Printed in the United States of America, North Mankato, Minnesota